Rhapsody

for

September

Rhapsody

for

September

Rhapsody for September

Love Letters

Rhapsody for September: Love Letters
©Doris Wellington 2007-2020
Dwelling Places Worldwide
Home of books and letters
By Doris Wellington
Georgia, USA

Unless otherwise noted
All scriptures taken from King James Version of the Bible
Public Domain
First US Copyright printing, 2020
Kindle Direct Publishing

Available on Amazon.com
and other online outlets

ISBN-13: 978-0998150772
ISBN-10: 0998150770

Cover Design
Doris Wellington

Dedication

I dedicate this work to my mother, Hattie Vance Wellington, with whom I shared a full life of mutual love, admiration, and joy for poetry. She not only taught me how to live, she showed me how to live with dignity and the pride of womanhood—that it doesn't matter how many times life knocks you down, you can get up dancing if you don't give up.

I honor you for what you gave me—earth life, unconditional love, nurture of soul, faith in God, freedom to dream, wings to fly, and the unbridled force of your determined resolve. This is your enduring legacy, which I don't take lightly.

Inside This Volume

In This Volume (Con't)

Introduction

<u>Rhapsody for September: Love Letters</u> was composed under various influences of love or what I believed so. They do not, however, represent any particular doctrine or construct held on the subject of love or how one must engage the emotions regarding it. Some of these letters are connected to specific relationships, others are not. The diverse nature of these writings show how the heart can be fashioned, caressed, and even shattered by words composed in the name of love. I only hope to show through these letters that God's love for me has multiplied my ability to love and has given me the strength and endurance needed when I have felt betrayed by love, or have myself betrayed love given from the heart and that the unconditional love that flows from the heart of God has forever affected how I see, engage, and give love.

It you are reading this book, it is my hope that you will find the love that shapes the heart into pure unadulterated joy—that you will not allow anything to sabotage your right and will to give love, whether it is the intimate love between husband and wife or the love of God that reaches across nations, peoples and tongues and illuminates all that the world lacks when love does not exist. It doesn't matter how many times the heart has been wounded and left bereft of song; it has been bestowed the greatest and profoundest of all life's mission—to love. Where there is love there is the will to forgive and love again. No one can teach the heart how to love a husband or wife, or anyone for that matter—only the heart that surrenders to the highest of all love can ever hope to know the power, purpose and joy of pure unselfish Love.

Where Love Finds Me

I want to speak of Love
Love that has eluded
Stalked
Chased
Resisted my advances
Love I bore
Absent
Of a suitable heart to possess it

Love that overpowered
And shifted between
Seasons of insanity
Holding on
And clinging to my
Irrationalities

I want to speak of love
But is this the place
Where I've spoken
Of your Holiness
And righteousness

Can I here speak
Of the carnal heart
That longs for more
Than I have given
For fear and regret

Absence of understanding
That it too needed care

Can I in the solace
Of a place rendered sacred
Mention that
Which is deemed only
Consumed in flesh

Must I here confess
Amid my holy convictions
That God's love suffices
When my carnal heart seeks
Love's refuge
To know
To hold
To be enraptured
Caught up
In a love given
By divine sanction
Or by consent of soul

The need
I have to sow
Into the heart of another
The volume of love
Withheld
Bound captive
To waiting
Denied

I'm here to testify
To lose the restraints
Of discipline
Abandon mores
Never mine
Witness silenced
By the solitude of
The Great Commission
Which I neither
Regret
Nor decry

I am neither a victim
Of misery
Nor scorn

I am a heart
Filled with what was given
Giving only that
Not taken by God
Not grudgingly
But willing
For willful was my decision

I Will Love Again

And again
But hurt shall never again
Hold captive my heart
I will love
And when it is over
I will release it to the wind
And love again
Never again shall pain
Pierce through
The core of my being
Leaving my heart
Barren of songs
That lovers sing
I will love
Then recycle the pain
Of untapped emotions
For the next time

For he who enters
The core of the being
Will surely come again
I dare not abandon
The vastness of heart
The pureness of soul
The promise of hope
To live without love
No
No
And No again

Man...Bye

My heart tried to give way to hurt
Amid the peace
I had only a few hours ago declared
Until he informed me
You must let me go
Cease to believe
In me
In us
As if I were for reasons he knew

Holding on to some delusion
That I couldn't bear
To let him go
Because he had decided
That we weren't meant
To be together

Forgetting perhaps
That it was I
Who first decided
That I wouldn't hold on
Without knowing to what

That I had no intention
His game to play
To be guided
By some misguided vice

Some undefined
Nowhere to go
Relationship
No end to know

So don't email
Text
Or ring my cell
Until you got some idea
Of where you're going

But I won't wait until
herewith
Man,,,
Bye!!!

Hush, Hush Sweet Nectar

Come, love
Hold me close
I wait in sweet surrender
Wrap your arms
Around my love
Whisper wind songs
Tender
Two hearts
One body
Intertwined
Like God
Must have envisioned
Love
Yielded
Without restraints
Of carnal pleasure
Or the thrill
Of temporary lust
That peaks
And disappears
Before flesh is satisfied

How long
I've waited
The strong coarse hands
Of your caress
Calming my fear
Claiming my love
Your own

How I've yearned
To release the elation
Of suppressed longing
And love
I've craved
For years to embrace

Pulling away
Seemed safer
More noble in God's eyes
For me to be chaste

Now the sun rises
There is no poetry
The days flee
There is no call

The night slips
Into another morning
And still I've not heard
Your voice
I miss what I love

I love what I miss
So, I pray everyday
For another chance
To hold you
And never let go
To love you
And never withhold

1Each passing hour
That we are apart
Multiplies my joy
To hold you again

Unveiled

Tell me about this man
You have allowed me to love
Others came nobler
Seemingly
More deserving

More gentry
Less common

Fitted to social standard
Tall
Debonair
Extremely
Charismatic

But he came
Wrapped in no disguise
No pretence
No portfolio
No intention
To beguile

Crude
Somewhat callous
Not as pleasing to the eye
Mantle tattered
By a fragile past
I saw a soldier
Down

We did not count on love
Not him
And certainly not I
Still
It became apparent
As time became days
And our twain hearts
Burst wide
To a fresh new
New opportunity
To love
And be loved

I criticized
Lord
I complained
He just didn't seem
My type

Our incompatibilities
Appeared
Insurmountable

But I loved his wit
He made me laugh
He thought me beautiful
He woke me with words
And rhyme
Like no one
Had before

He doted on me
And pleaded with God
Jehovah, Father
God
If I have done anything right
Please make this woman
Mine

I want to be the one
She loves
The one she holds at night
My heart
My soul
Will honor
Her
And serve her
Every desire

She's one among
A fading breed
She did not
Just appear
She came
After many days
I believe
She is my gift
You brought her
To me
A bit naïve
Not worldly in any way
She seeks the good
In every one
She found the good
In me

I have travelled
Around the world
Three times

I have returned
She is all I've ever wanted
All
I've waited for

Give me your love
Your heart
Your hand

Give me your pledge
To marry
Make me your trusted
Husbandman
I'll walk the straight
And narrow

He loved me into loving him
With proclamations
And prayer
He would not yield
Until I promised
That we would
Be one flesh

Watch and see
He would always say
I want you as my wife
My love
My friend
My bride

Father,
You knew
My determined resolve
My take on love and life
That at my age
I do not have
Time to sacrifice

He's years my junior
I wonder if it matters
I have the experience
Of relationship
He has the gift of banter

He has the children
I am barren
My earth womb has not borne
Still we could not hope to be
Unless we moved us forward

But when he reached for me
I moved away
I pushed the more
He pulled
Years of broken
Promises
Had left me
Somewhat numb

He did not uncover me
I did not dishonor you
I did not abandon principle
We made no fleshly truce
I have not been
Less your daughter

I haven't been defiled
Holding myself for the one
Who'll take me as his bride

If it doesn't offend you
I offer this condition
If this is not to be the one
this page will be my witness

I do not will a change of mind
I'll gladly wait the promise
Those who enter hearts by choice
Hold no fear of tomorrow
Just love me I pray
Through summer's long
Let no winter ever pass
If hearts must wait like nature's bloom
Let them wait with song

Still Comes My Love

I hold my breath
My heart still yearns
It does not rest
Behind the mask
Of unrequited love
I am flushed
But not ashamed
That dream has not left me
The heart is obstinate
Naked and

 Refused in youth
Womanhood profaned
Behind the mask of manhood
And the seal of marriage
And the cross they say Jesus bore
I bore in glossolalia
Eli Eli la'ma'sabach'thani

Someday eyes will read
And souls will render me barren
Presume me to be naïve
Or dismiss me all together
But regarding love
I'm inscrutable

Craving like a woman with child
Hungry as one who has for forty days
and nights
Abstained from food

Presume me fool, but
Judge me not
Twice widowed
Still filled with promise
Desire never wilted
Skin supple to the touch
Beauty never surrendered
Loins still pregnant with love
For the husband I never married
I see him in wakening
And in sleep I imagine
That he waits for me
Until at last
He comes

Where is he
I await his touch
Against my body
Still pliable to give that
Withheld from another

Gentleman and ghoul
Hearts rejected fail waiting
Repelled by love I could not give
For it belonged to one

How I love him still
Who is he and
When will he appear?

For certain
They who are dead
Cannot return again
To the living to love

Where Love Leads

Fierce arrows
Transform into peaceful darts
Before they reach
Their destination
And are consumed by the air
That held steady their trajectory
Behind the cosmic force
That countersigned their defeat
Mission aborted
Heart left intact
The decision to love
Greater than the conspiracy
To not

Perhaps he didn't want my love
Rather
Just the fantasy
The mystery and allure
Of an elusive lover
The rapturous pursuit of the forbidden
That has grown
Strange fruit in winter

The impetuous hunt
With no real purpose for the prey
Except
To cast it back into the wilds
Once it has been trapped

Perhaps we loved
But were not as convinced
Of that love
As when we first met

Oh but the heart did bleed
From the image in the mirror
Starring back
Convincing me
That love is possible
At any age

Perhaps the fear of loving
So convinced of loving
Grafted fear
And pushed back the yearning
That flamed the fire

Perhaps there being
Neither fire nor passion
Just longing
To temporarily
Abate the loneliness

That leaves the heart
Hoping
To bridge the soul
To that which it still seeks to find
That which
Only festers full bloom in season

Perhaps he needed the courage
To love again
As I
Who once declared
That my shop of such feelings
Was closed forever
Without the minimal possibility
Of a beneficiary
To claim the bounty
Of suppressed desire

No offers accepted
No negotiations
All proposals denied

My heart takes only prisoners
Only prisoners need apply
The door locks from without
There is no key from inside

Perhaps we stumbled into a night
Lit each other's path
Until our tunnel
Was filled again with hope
That only love can engender
So we walked surreally
Hand in hand
Laughter potent
And potions

From rising
Until other work
Claimed our attention
And we
reluctantly turned
To answer

Was it love
I shall know
Sooner I pray
Than later
Whether the heart
Can truly shut down
And make no more demands
Upon its vast potential to bind
Without restraints

I have not
But so draught with longing
Desire
Love without hugging caution
That mortifies
The purest of God's
Treasures

To love without pause
Not like those
Whose love lives
Have long dwarfed
By capitulation

Love
Without abstract consideration
Of fear
Which does not exist
Unless I give it form

I want to love
And be loved
As freely a man
As I have loved God

Perhaps
He thought himself
Not good enough
For a God woman
Whose goodness
He felt compelled to praise
In every conversation

Perhaps
He felt not righteous enough
For her purity
Not pious enough
For how could he
Compete with God?

This good God woman
Who sought the same
In everyone

And never failed
To speak her God purpose
With passion
And vociferous praise

Perhaps his love
Fell short
With inadequacies
Often reminded
By criticism
Of short coming
Looking into the face
Of what he believed
Near perfection
Was just the veil behind
Which I pleaded
For some conviction of self
To remove the façade
Behind which I wept
For a savior

A man-savior
Not God
For I have been saved
From sins I shall never commit
Unless someone
More egotistical than I
Transgress
My pretentious sublimity
To be chaste

To commit my purest yearnings
To the most trusting heart
Unembellished in his arms
Without feeling
That somehow I'm cheating God

Who has given all love
Without hording
And seeks only
That it be transferred
To one capable
Of giving it the glory
Of original purpose

To calm the rancor of life
From the dragging of storm
And anchor the soul
Against irreverent and aberrant
Alarm

To balance the emotions
Without binding the spirit
Too temperate
To emancipate the forbidden
Which could be
The harbinger
Of the spirit's call to disarm

To know the truth
And to desire that truth
For the freedom that claims
The core of imprisoned desire
Only to be denied
Because
Understanding fails as
To the purpose of God

If you shall know the truth
And the truth will make you free
Why is my man still bound
In chains
Reserved for those captive
To religious pretention
Who think more highly
Of their own prowess
Than he thinks of God
Or me

Isn't God more eternal
Than the breaking away of hearts
Can he not hold steady
The uncertainty that lurks

Is not he God-capable
Of steering the intemperate
Passions to the highest
Realization of love

And
Who'll pay less attention
To my pious shield
And more to the perishing
Of famished desire

Which I too have crucified
And hanged bare upon a cross
To lie entombed
Until love
Resurrects me whole

I wait
For I am certain
My latter will be greater
And I too
Shall be enraptured
In the glory of that
Denied

If there is such an answer
I want to know
I need to know
I pray to know

My soul waits
But the answer
Does not come swiftly
And hope
Consumes me with perhaps…

I have walked among the dead living
Toiling to be
But not fully succeeding
I'm not dead
I am alive
Breathing the malignancy
Of rejection
Rejecting the malignancy
Of breathing
Simply because
He doesn't understand
That I'm more needy than he
More needy
Than my desire for flesh
I need him to lead

I Will Follow

I'll go with him
Fraught with folly
Like there is no now
That's waits tomorrow
For he who sees me
Behind the mask of the sacred
Is trustworthy
For he has penetrated the songs
And saintly ways
Of those in need of salvation

So convinced am I
That such a man exists
I plant a seed
For his manifest

I don't need a man-god to worship
I'm not a goddess to seek
That yearning I have fulfilled
In my Father

I seek the purest form in man
To challenge my womanhood
Above the wrestling
Of condemnation
And strength of will to bow

No less a woman
Endowed to give
The deepest part of me
Belonging to man
Transgressing not
Against my God

I vow to devote affection
Reserved
For the enchantment
Of true love
 I think I've found
In him

If it is not to be
I will not wither
I will not die

I have dared to love
Again and again
And with that be satisfied
That I'm not dead
I am alive

Hope streaming
Like rivers
I have loved
And shall love again
Until found

The heart equipped
And entitled to endure
The crush of waves
The dashing of tides

Is not at fault when decided
"It's best to have loved and lost
Than not to have loved at all"
And yet I know

Within these hallowed places
Love is never lost
it is recycled
To give to another
In greater measures than before
To spend its gift
Upon the deserving
Is just as noble
When it is not returned

Confessions

To love those
Who cannot love
I stand before a cradled dream
Nurtured by divinity
I'm the victor
I chose to love
To waltz in its splendor
To communicate
The highest pleasure
Between mortal bodies
Immortalizing moments
Held in eternity
Long past
Orgasmic pleasure

To embrace the ethereal
The pain that confirms
That love has existed

No less a woman
No more a fool
Than those whose feet
Venture to walk
The only path
That multiplies itself
In spite of failure

There's none suited
None who deserves
The infinite devotion of true love
That gives without reservation
Or unsupported admiration
No portfolio required
For the unconditional

So entering with knowledge
That the heart sometimes
Leads unwise
Gives pause
To whether it's wise
To love at all
Without reciprocation
Then perhaps
Love becomes a stranger
Locked behind its own walls

I confess
I've been there
I've carried the waste
Of love overhaul
With nowhere to store the excess
Except behind wounds
And scar tissue that wouldn't heal
Or bitterness
Seeking asylum behind regrets

Trying to vaccinate my desires
From affections I decline
Refusing to become a robot
Guarding the heart
Against life
Brain dead
Instructing the emotions
To shut down
At the first sign of romantic intent
Remain plutonic
Play safe the game
Where victims cower
Prisoners to heartbreak

Vowing never again
To take the plunge
Or the risk and dare
Of those who love
With or without the pain

Albeit dangerous
I prefer love
Above the tryst of hate
I burst wide open
To build the bond
Between strangers
Who meet

Knowing nothing of the other
Both granted a blank canvas
Upon which to write
To build a house
Where the mortal heart dwells

Or bake a cake
From scratch
The playing field
Revealed by ignorance
Or the sharing
Of innocent desire

One motive
One interlocking drive
To go where the heart leads
And leads where hearts have been denied

There love will find me
There I will rise
To fondle its call
Pouring all of my intimate response
Into the cup of salvation
To answer whether I can love
As deeply in flesh as spirit
As I can without it either

Is it possible that bonds of love
Birthed in the heart
Are strengthened by the body
Blood giving life to the flesh
Not flesh giving life to blood
Sexual hording without the benefit
Of heart
Deprives the soul of friendship

Judge me naive
Loving under diminished capacity
Ask me
How much hurt the heart can take
Before it is emasculated
And deemed unfit
To engage in reproductive desire

Ask me if love can fail
If so
How incompetent is God
To put such power
Into the hands of mere mortals
To abuse

When love is his mantle
It has turned the curse of nations
Birthed the antidote against hate
And filled
The vacuum of nuances
Emptied by pernicious evil

Love abides the only true axiom
Teach me that truth
And I will wait
Hoping against hope
For that day
When all the love I have given

Absolutely
Without resentment
Shall return to me
In one lump sum
And love me
As I have loved

Before I extirpate
All hope of finding
What I thought I had
And perhaps I have
God help me
I thought I had

So I will wait
To love and be loved
Like the river
That enters quietly
And empties itself into the deep
Like the rhythm of a flawless waltz

Dance with me
Until satisfied
Or until Winter turns Spring
Or Spring September
I have loved
And God willing
I shall love again

Husband

I love you like
Thinking
But drawing no definitive
Conclusion
To what you want
Like abstract
Amorphous lines
With no defined construct

I love you
Like aimless moving
Towards no planned
Destination
To please
Like rancorous
Rebellion
With no cause
To rally support

But the heart
Inciting debauchery
Possessing no plan
To redirect it
Like lost
Compass broken
No turning point
To anchor
The thrust of spontaneity
Overflowing
Into malignant passion

Follow my heart
To the land of milk and honey
Where the holiest of water
Mingled with blood
Bear witness to our spirit

We are one
In ways that others
Shall never experience
And thus two hearts fitly joined
Can manifest love's highest pleasure
To cast the body into the prison
Of another's desire

I want to embrace
Without fear
The one
Who anticipates my longing
And gently responds
Accordingly

If the one I love
Desires my arms
I am yours
You are mine
We will surrender
To the other
The deepest of the journey
It takes time
So be patient
And love will take us there

Through the rugged plains
Made smooth
Where love
Can feast
And I shall bar no access
As you have made you fully mine

Love me
With passion's
Abandoned conventions
 Possess me now
As I am yours
Our love no longer
Needs defining
The wind
The bird
The sun
The sky
Say it all
It took a lifetime to devour
Such desire

I will love you quietly
Until the last symphonic echo
Fades into the acoustics of the air
I will love you as loudly
As the cacophonic overture
Of nature allows
I will love you
Pensive
And out loud
To dancing
And to no music at all

Pursue Me Like a Warrior

You entered my world
Without permission
Resolute
Determined
Unpretentious
Barring
Any present
Or unforeseen resistance
You came in a champion
No flags raised
In surrender
Needed
You are a warrior
Prove
That warrior blood
Runs through your veins
Pursue me
Unafraid

Dear You

I had not planned on loving you
No more than you planned to love me
I simply wanted your laughter
Your constant presence
And unadulterated truth
Perhaps more than you know
God answered your prayer
And to my delight
He answered mine

I was lonely
You saved me from episodic
Loneliness
I felt confined
You freed my soul
To longing again
I was in need of man love
You gave me yours
You fed my soul
from your plenty
My heart runs over

For me
It was surprising
That I would allow myself
Open my heart
And allow you passage

When we met
There was a great gulf
Between our incompatibilities

But now I find myself in love
Not with one deemed
Suitable
But in love with you
If your father were here
He would know
Right from the start
That my love is true
No one falls for a jagged rock
Unless she knows for sure
That a diamond lurks
Somewhere inside

So, do not talk yourself out of me
For I have talked myself into you
The playing field is leveled
Let's stay together
Let's prove that love
Can birth the strangest desire
And still endure
The strangest difference
And still be compatible

Pull me into your manly presence
Caress me with the warmth of body
Inhume the aura of my womanly
That presses every inch of me
Into your loving
Begging with my desire
Every fiber of my being
Wanting you
Giving to you
What I til now withheld
If you can believe it
You could be the love of my life
Or the beneficiary
Of some default of time
When I heap
All repressions
And fantasies
On one lucky guy

Simply because
I've never been free enough
Or cared enough
or believed I could love someone
Totally and fully enough
To give myself
Uninhibited

You
My love
Could be in trouble
It must be a burden to know
You could be the one
To reap the excess
Of all my longing

No one has even written me
Into the journal of their desires
Until you
Take me into your arms
Cup your lips around my soul
I am your wife
Caress me
Until my reluctance give way
To trust

What I do not know
I yield to your leading
Trusting your gentleness
To guide my innocence
Protect my surrender
And take me where
Only love can enter
Where no imposter
Has the key to

Where no hands
Has ever left me
Hopeless
Or helpless to his mercy
I want to be loved by you
I want to be the one
To whom
You pledge your body
I am your wife

Or, are you afraid
Is that your story
Were you afraid
That first day I saw you?

You spoke as though
You had no worries
Quiet and confident
You walked on water
You stepped right into
The midst of my heart
No invitation
You didn't even knock

Why did you choose me unafraid
Did I appear easy to convince
Was I fragile
And hard to figure
Or just a project
To indulge your curiosity

Love me as one who loves forever
Brush your hands along
The length of my body
Push back the fears
Though gently

Leave me fulfilled
Or do not
Touch me at all

Funny Heart Love

Lord
I just thought of something funny
I know you saw that man coming
There was Perry
And Smith
To date I just don't get it
Why him?
Was I set up?
If so...
By whom
I sure hope you don't say
The devil
Because if it were
I would've changed my order
But as it stands
The heart has fallen
Now I question
Whether disappointed

Doris Wellington

I dreamed him
Tall and debonair
He dwarfed my expectations
But when he found me
I thought
Height is overrated

But given my fickle history
Of choosing men for love
Why didn't you warn me sooner
Why didn't you give me word
I would have never chosen him
Except by consent of spirit
If by lust of the eye
Lord
I truly missed it

He surely does not qualify
For his material position
Leaves less to be desired
Than being short in statue
Still he offered me
The tender of his heart
If I would surrender mine
Perhaps we could move forward

Love me whole
I surrender
To you
I offer my heart
For years of barren
Withholding
Perhaps
It's not love at all
But the years of pain
And sorrow

He chose to yield
To make me laugh
Calling certain times of day
Indulging me in his folly
He begged to have his say
The very thing that I had missed
A tonic for the lonely
For years I prayed for this day
I yearned to be held closer

He came
Giving what he had
Compliments
Common poetry
He was
The perfect
Gentleman

But Criticizing
And complaining
Was all
That I could offer

No force of will to bind the heart
Forever
Pure and simple
I wasn't ready
For the strings
That tied me
To his future
I only wanted
The warmth of being
To hold me for the moment
Until the lonely was abated
And the wounds were mended

When transparency
Unveils itself
To hypocrisy
It penetrates the core of truth
There is no pretention
At least I can't discern it

He spoke without protecting
His man code
Contrived in the cave
Of like minded

I love you every day
The way you wear your hair
Your smell
Your quirky laugh
And sunshine ways

I love the way you move
Sauntering
Gliding about
Sitting down like the quiet of dawn
I love your quick wit
Knowing how to handle yourself
Classic slick

I love your heart
Your funny eyes
I love to see you come
Can't wait to see you turn around
So I can watch you go
You're the right everything
The right size
The right height
The right coke body physique
The right mixture of yellow and brown
The right sense
Of who you are

It took years to become
The person you are
Let no one spoil it now
I only want you and what you give
Nothing less or more

He spoke volumes
To my womanhood
To the longing of my heart
But I stood by
Judging his truth
Refusing to give in to lust

You only want what is yours
I only want what is mine
The wind swept across our pledges
Like a breeze out of time
The thrust of the storm
Beat vehemently against our door
Adversity stood between us
Threatening to the core
But we held fast
Our funny love
To get here
Where we are

Unhinged

The man looked
First at me
Then at her
Staring
Piercing up and down
Through and through
Back and forth
Like the point guard
In the final minute
Of a tied game

Who will be the first to score
Her
Or her
I feel his manhood wrestling
With the possibilities
They're both so different

His heart races
With contemplative lust
Pounding
Shifting his indecisiveness
From foot to foot

Pacing between stolen glances
Rationalizing

Perhaps
One of them has pulled him
Into her thoughts
To lie with him
Or to him
Pretending
Fantasying
Eye to eye
Heart to heart
Groins vibrating
Racing against the clock
No words stir
Just sensual arousal
Hopeful gazes
Fornication in the mind

He must make his move
They will soon leave
One of them
Or both

He caresses their wind blown hair
Flying upward without restraints
He cast a wistful moment
Into the atmosphere
Then moves consumed by lust

Hands cupping the crouch
Pulsating to the rhythm
Of lascivious desire

There is no time to waste
No time to consider the outcome
He takes the plunge
And quickly passes
Her
Without as much as a nod
Acknowledging
Her existence
Or casting his eye

As he nears me
I realize
I have been chosen

I fluff my disheveled hair
Connecting with his eyes
To convey interest
Then walk purposely
In the opposite direction
To my car
I will make this easy for him
By reducing his possibilities
To none

Spoiler

January 27, 2013

I was the spoiler
I penned the leaven
Women borrowed
To spellbound their lovers
From the inkwell of potions
Scribbled across paper
And passed along as anecdotes
For the love sprung

Intimate portraits
Eroticism
Wrapped in linen
And silk spice
Then poured upon the object
Of one's desires
Pen oozing with passion poison
Nothing hailed me greater
Nothing gave me more delight
Than to be the conduit to hearts
And souls bursting with desire
The love struck quoted me
Used my name without a fee
Violated my inner thoughts
Became the me I could not be

I lived their lives
They lived their dreams
All their fantasies
Flowed from my pen

I captured my prey
In verse and rhyme
Meticulous to a fault
Then I ran and hid
My hand
And left the vain
In awe

I poured my heart
Upon paper
That bled lonely
Between the lines

When all I ever really wanted
Was to be loved
Without hyperboles
Or Lies
While others enjoyed
What I created

I wrapped my heart
In metaphoric language
In textbook literary form
I freed them to love
While I walked alone
In perfect
Lines
Between the pages
Of their lives

Who Am I?

Would you still love me
If I were a clone
If all that you see
Were not me born
What if my hair was fake
My eyes were contacts
My lips just Botox
And my breast were implants
That the thing that makes me
Swivel and move
Had been carefully designed
To hide my flaws
Would you still love me
If my smile were cut and paste
Clip art
My voice a downloaded ring tone
And
My heart the fragments
Of an accident gone wrong
And all that you see
Was not me at all

Would you still love me
If I were a clone
Genetically engineered
In a scientific loam
My flawless complexion
Chanel and Fashion Fair
A Mary Kay facial
Or a Revlon mask
Would you still love me
If my fingernails and lashes
Were mere pull offs
And all that you see
Were not DNA at all

But this is just a poem
With no power over me
I am as real a woman
As real can be
I bruise and bleed
Laugh and cry
Feel hurt and pain
Live and die
I hope and pray
And dream the future
What you see
Is not an illusion

Knoxville

Our meeting
Though brief
Was pleasant

I laid my head upon your shoulder
You gave my toil rest

Few words passed between us
Even fewer than I remember

Though strangers
Friends we parted
The memory
Still lingers

You to Knoxville
Me—
I'm not certain

My days and nights
Of now and then
Run their course together

We never called
Or spoke thereafter
We never belonged
Together

Just one fleeting moment in time
We shared our personal narratives
Wherever you are
Still I am
This itinerate missionary

The sun by day
The moon by night
Embracing battle weary

But harder to forget than distance
Is the erasure of the image
1968 or '69
I left it unaffected

A thousand questions left behind
A thousand times revisited
Who was the man sitting next to me
Intrusive and inquisitive

A long gold hooded maxi
An afro
Moved and shaped by times
Platform shoes
Jeans and jewelry
A beige satin blouse
Contagious laughter
Engaging eyes
A million dollar smile

A stretch of road
Between two hearts
Two destinies
Intertwined

I hope
Somewhere between
The stops
Of youthful
Aimless travel
You found the soul
That binds the heart
To the promise
Of forever

This is it

It secures
And shatters
At the heart's core
And beneath well protected
Layers of denial
Or glaring surface allure

Illusive
Unbridled
Rejected
Or
Delirium
Morbid demure

Priggish
Panache
Squeamish
Bold
Embraced
Forbidden
Sensual
Savage
Seductive
Mystical force

Ecstasy
Ethereal
Mistaken for
Remorse

Against winds of adversity
Against the grains of tradition
Or family history
Without agreeable
Discussion
Of suitability

Moving without compass
Driven by instinctive conditions
For which medicine
Has no cure
Or no recovery of diagnostic
Tendencies
Or symptoms
Too late to treat
Or advise

Burning desire
Cast into beds of iniquity
Caution aside

Walking to the altar
Of matrimony
Beaming with
Prenuptial wisdom
Or fears
Of distrust

Lost innocence
Puppy indulgence
Eyes filled with laughter
Or suspicious
Lust

Thrust upon the
Undeserving
For wounds
Gone by
For indulging the heart
In reckless abandon
Or reason
Hidden
Behind the veil
Of captives
Forsaking all
To honor one
Pledging youth
And ageless hearts

Seeking solace
Feverishly

Investing emotions
Never thought existed
Creating chaos
Amid a world of serenity
Forcing strength

Exposing the weakness
Of children barely born
Incapable
Of making decisions
That bind the soul
Before it can repent

Or binds the body
To blood ties
That will never be broken

Just stored
In vaults
Of hope
Recycled or reborn

Daring to trust again
In spite of
Because of
Instead of
Loveless living
Driven by hate
Yearning
To destroy

Or permit wounds
To turn to rottenness
And bitterness
Scar tissue
That salves cannot sooth
Or no instrument
Mend
By the keenest of precision

So we move on
Where fools do enter
The revolving door
That swings to the right
And left
Threatening to entrap
Its victim

But must
By reason of entering
Free them to love
With one toss about
And turn
Of choice

Endowed with new zeal
New possibilities
A new thought
Derived
From weeks
And months
Years
Of therapy
For another chance
At love

Casting long gazes
And quick glances
Across the room
Filled with hilarity
Boisterous and unruly joy
Moving closer
Shoulder to shoulder
Leaning inward
And nipping at ears

Toasting to the hope
Of making plans
For the future
Or where to spend
New Year's Folly
If all goes well

Restraints relaxed
Fears abandoned
To pleasure

Scintillating
Emasculating
Fervent laughter
That fills
A vacuum
Without electricity

Sheer happiness
Born in the midst
Of shared propensities
And commonalities
That resist
Mundane
Silliness

Born again
Converted
Renewed
Revived
Living out loud again
In spite of yesterday
Alive
To the sound of music
The rustling of leaves
The whispering
Of windblown nature
Alive

Unmoved
 By the cacophony of streets gone wild
The silence of night
The bustle of work
The aloneness of the moment

For it's only temporary
Until the cell rings
The doorbell blasts
Or the text lights up

Or the ipod
And endless new tech gadgets
Alert to
One missed call
Or new message

Waiting
Or blogs
That internet affords

Alive to even the
Time consuming method
It takes
To say hello
I only have a minute
That turns to an hour
Or an hour that lasted beyond
Journals
Notepads
And listening

Thoughtfulness
That says in the gesture
What words cannot

Metaphors
A lifetime guarantee
To arouse sentiments
Or sadness

Roses
Diamonds
Cologne
Perfume
Of a certain preference
That lingers beyond the last squirt

Sharing best kept secrets
That quiet restaurant
 Tucked in the middle of oblivion
Or a romp in the park
That merry-go round shopping experience
Exhausted
Sipping from the same straw
Devouring the same air
Inhaling a lifetime of germs
Through two conjoined hearts

Adoring
Immersed in
Mindless living
Absent from the body
Idolizing mortality
Suspended in time
Day standing still
Every moment passing swiftly

As garments are
Gingerly removed
Or torn away like beasts
Seeking prey

Holding captive
Whispering in tongues
Careless to disrupt

Biting
And secreting lust
With exquisite words
Created to caress the flesh
Flushed against flesh
Heart pounding
Against the silence of night
Or the rancor of day

Refusing to deny
Any expression
Of delight
Or passionate concord

Compromising
Accommodating
Spending the last
Saving for that rainy day
That surprise
Birthday
Anniversary
Or special vacation
Sanity slipping
Between alternate realities

Sweet
Bitter
Joy
Sorrow
High
Low
Uncertain
More than certain

Sacred song
Serenading to the rejoice
Of spirit
And the repose
Of soul

Who am I
To whom do I belong
And why
Is it alright to assume
That this is love

Who labeled the lust
For carnality
The pursuit of happiness?
Who has drawn the lines
Between passionate surrender
And teasing of flesh

Through sleepless nights
And peaceful drifting
Into the reveries of dawn
That meet the sun's
Good morning kiss

Beholding a serenity
Never experienced
An awareness of simple
Miracles

The serenade of birds
The brush of the wind
The rustle of leaves beneath the feet

The rise and fall of seasons
Without fail
Without apology
The synergy between
Moon and sun

Wonders of splendor
Heretofore ignored
Now one symphonic chord of beauty
One unbroken cord of truth

One purifying thought
That flows throughout the being

The tingling sensation of life
That grips the soul's core
Demanding its response
To the gift being given

The relentless knocking
Upon the heart
That will not cease
Until it is opened

Enters the irrevocable
Myth and magic
Truth and lore
Proverbial
Syntax
Of a language
Spoken only in the code
Of two

No translation
Except the heart
No third party
Intruders

Just one endless door
That leads to the
Inner chamber
The Sanctum Santorum

The sacred alter
Upon which is cast
The eternal oblation

The only sacrifice
That endures
The only investment
That multiplies itself
In one way or another
The moment it is given
 And received

The ultimate possession
The greatest of all human emotions
The end of all expectations
There is nothing that rivals
In waiting
No plan of salvation
That secures the soul
More than its precious
Allure
Its power
Its provocative demeanor
Its infinite arms
Intoxicating

What a dream
What splendor
What fairytale?

Such fanciful sacrifice
To have and to hold
Until death
Or a sudden interruption
Of a nightmare
Snatching away
The expectation
Of growing old
And having grandchildren

Then
Suddenly
Silently
Without notice
Or concern
For the delicate tissue of the heart

Burning like a ferocious
Fire
Without warning
Debilitating
Overwhelming
Consuming the natural
Balance
And course of days coming
Unhinged

An affair
A one night fling
A bet
An angry impulse
A misunderstanding
Perpetuated
By stubbornness
Pride
Gnawing away reasoning

Vindictive
Using love to recompense anger
To make amends
Fire with fire
Out of control
Until there's no way
To retrieve the words
Spoken out of the vortex of indifference

Over and over
To redundancy
And nuisance fixation

Hatred spewed out
Spilling over
Wasted emotions

Repenting
But not really
Desiring
But without senses
To lead
Down the path of regret
And reconciliation

Given all
Taken all
Bent over
Bent down
Trying to fix with a bandage
What surgery can't

Counseling
Therapy sessions
For losers
Last only for then
And so
They walk
Hapless
Alone
Reminiscing
Retrieving memories
Saved
In the archive of bliss

Pondering
Contemplating
Is this one worth saving?

How much this time
Am I willing to invest
How much can I tolerate
Until there's nothing left

Walking
Jogging
To relieve the aching
Considering making the call
Then flips the script

Praying for possibilities
And alternatives
That don't exist

It was only a fling
Meaningless
I didn't mean it to turn into this
Should have left
Before the lights flicked to amber
Should have left the office
As soon as he called
Was it a call for help

I could've resisted
Had I not been so sure
I had this
After all
I'm in control of myself

I have a good woman
Getting up 5: O'clock to get to work
She's a jewel

One mistake
And I'm ready to call it quits
When in fact
I know her loyalty
She stood up to her dad for me
She wouldn't take down
She believed in me then

I believe in her now
Just a young lady when we met
Fragile
Holding on to my every word
She clung to my promise
To prove her love

What went wrong
We're strong
We're better than this

We made a vow
To honor
And there are no cowards
Where honor is concerned
She's my baby
My best friend
She always has my back

One cup of coffee
We shared it
One piece of bread
We blessed it
And broke it in half
Between us

Sharing the last dollar
The last word
Designing our days
Around the dream
We sought

We were hopeful
Pregnant with great ideas
Empowered by oneness
Future multiplied in children
Carried
Proudly
Father and son
Mother and daughter

Family
Changing the world
By our conviction to be
Friends
Lovers
Partners
Leaders
Witnesses
Peacemakers
Instruments of God
Keepers of generations
Hands that save
What others can't

Eyes beholding
Pureness
Grace
Mercy
Redemption
Forgiveness
Reconciliation

This time
I will fight

Hopeful

I will find you
Or you will find me
And the great love shared between us
Will be rekindled
And there will be dancing
In the streets
The summer of 1989
Shall repeat
In multiplied portions
To compensate
For loss

No apologies
Will be necessary
Forgiveness will be complete

Laughter
Abject
And malignant
Shall cling to the roof
Of the head
And heal
The laceration of soul

And all of London
Shall dance with us

Behind the Mask of Perfection

The alarm chimes to
"It's a man's world"
Not a minute later or earlier
Than half past six am

He leans over
And whispers
 In the corner of Susie's ear
Ten minutes to breakfast he chirps
And disappears
With perfect strides
Behind corridors
And winding hallways
To his private bath to shower and shave

She waves at her husband of sixteen years
Then pulls the lush silk around her waist

The Black and Decker
Percolates
A robust blend of cappuccino
To musical footsteps
Romping from room to room
Gently retrieving socks
From their color coded spaces

It's Monday
Brown tones with gold accents
No grays or blacks
It's just that simple

Ten minutes is quickly shaven
From his time
And he begins the countdown to one hour

In forty minutes he'll step into
The driver's seat
Of his luxury sports toy
And drive the twenty minutes around
Layham Parkway
To his penthouse office complex

Ten minutes to park
Before walking into his pristine
Corner office
At 7:20 promptly
His daily feat
Without delay

Like a classical work of art
He calls his wife
And arouses the children

He scrambles eggs
And pours the cereal
Pops wheat bread
Into the toaster
Sits at the head of the table
And showcases his power

He thumps a tiny crumb
From his place setting
And taps the glass
With his spoon
Reminding them
Whose in charge

In less than five minutes
A minuet of tiny feet
Parade onto the veranda
And navigate their way
Through the breakfast muse
With a husband kiss
And a father's hug
He's gone

Lingering slows his schedule
Interrupts the rhythm
Of perfection

He grabs the paper
From the mat
Then brandishes the remote
To his jeep
For all the hating neighbors
To seethe
Then just to irritate their envy
He changes his mind
And takes the Benz
Then he's off
Schedule intact

The day goes
As meticulously as planned
By a perfectionist of minor details

He instructs his assistant
To bring him coffee
Like a Chihuahua
On a short leash
She reads his calendar
And adjusts his loosely knotted tie

He briefs his staff
On the rise and fall of stocks and bonds
Then slides into his swivel throne
Behind the mahogany and bronze desk
Of dignitaries

No room for error
Or mayhem
No reason for stress
No BS

No Plan B necessary

Lunch at Downie's Grill
For a Rueben on rye
And chocolate milk
A leisure stroll across the park

A brief check of emails
And a quick call to his Admin
To inform her
He's running late
Any early appt will have to wait
A few short minutes

He closed the deal
With Swarthmore's
Checked the growth
Of his personal investments
Took on five new clients
In just under a week

Perfection shouldn't be so easy

At close of business
He begins the reverse ritual
To Hawthorne Trail
Avoiding the rash
Of rush hour rage

He arrives promptly
Half-past 6:00 PM

He kisses the children
Hugs the wife
Retreats to his private gym
Before the Faisons arrive for dinner

He entertains them
Until half past nine
Without fail
Then bids them good-night

Except tonight
He changes into a starter
And joggers
He yells to Susie
I'm off for a run

He waves as his longtime friends
Turn the corner
At the end of Havelock
Then he makes a U-turn
And enters through the patio door
Which he knows isn't locked
Because it never is

He gingerly removes his saddle leather shoes
Then tiptoes around the library
His wife feet rest against an ottoman
She's lost
In The Solitary Lives of Women in Peril

He pulls the revolver from his jacket
And with one bullet to the head
He fells his childhood sweetheart
She collapses upon the Persian Rug

Along her next intended read
The Myth of Marital Bliss

He left by the outer gate
Around the pool
Past the greenhouse
Along the lake

There were no sounds
The Golden Retriever was silent
The security alarm was disengaged
The children slept in their rooms
In the West end of the family estate

And the man waltzed freely into the night
Alibi as impeccable as life
Nothing to tie him to the crime
No blood DNA
No weapon found

Just the mask of discipline
And an empty shell casing
Near a handwritten note
The woman had dropped
Asking her husband
For a divorce

The handcuffs are as noisy
As his facade

Love Letters
from Vietnam

The Death of Love
That Day
Whose Fight Is It?
Vietnam Stole My Tom
Breached
Last Letter From Vietnam

The Death of Love

February 10, 2008

I do not love you anymore
I cannot love you anymore
Neither love I me
I will not love you if I return
To sanity
Or another altered state of being
 As close as I am to home
I don't love the coming
I hate a man
I cannot see

I kill children bearing arms
 Waiting

I'm utterly consumed by hate
That deprives of the will to love
I kill and torch
And to eulogize my remorse
I torch and burn sacred scorn
And bury its memory in ashen grief

I cannot love you
Not even me
I'm dispossessed of being
Loveless
Punished

That Day

The day you left
I remember it well
Your shaky hands placed gently in mine
The highest duty to the call of man
To defend his country from all enemies
You were but a ruddy youth
We had not long been together
With so much hope and promise before us
Eighteen and green
I had no understanding of such things
No thought to offer
Nothing above the comfort of loyalty
And the love
We held together

We held each other for an eternity
Declaring our hearts
I will wait until

We will write letters
As if you were here
Or I were there
It is after all temporary

My faith is strong
You are a dutiful man
With long life before you
You will return
I know it

Upon the honor of our love
And the glory of country
You will be valiant and austere
No enemy can penetrate such fortress
No weapon formed
Shall prosper against us
Hold fast our dream
Lie gingerly down each night
With me pressed against your pillow
As I will you
Praying
With thoughts lifted up
For your peace and safe

I will wait
Go onward soldier and fight
You are bound to honor
And serve your commander in chief
I cannot keep you from it
It will not keep you from me

To all that is truth and more glorious
I will set my soul to tomorrow
And turn forward time
Until then
I will wait my love
Until then
I will wait

Whose Fight is This?

Three days ago you arrived
On soil that is not yours
To fight a war that you didn't start
Or have no idea the conflict behind it all
Princess asked
Why is dad gone to fight?
What did Vietnam do to him?
And why can't those
who passed the first blow
Fight for themselves
It doesn't concern us
Does it?

I formed words
Fragmented explanations
That didn't register clear
But I must admit
I too am in the dark
I watched Walter Cronkite reporting live
As yet I held no letter from you

I do not know where you've camped
Or how you managed your flight
So write soon
And we will know how best to answer
Regarding this war

Vietnam Stole My Tom

I have no pictures of the prom I missed
Or photos that crowned my sister "Miss it."
The bell of the ball she had it all
Curves and hair that made me spit

I have no images to recall
How she stole TP from under my nose
While this ugly duckling sat content
In the ultimate space
Of gooficity

I have no still solemn photography
Of how our men went to war
In Vietnam just before
She and my boyfriend quit
And I moved on to taller things
More debonair a bit more lean
Then off to honor and defend
The patriotism of countrymen
They both were sent

Two gallant soldiers they went
Hers and mine

Neither inclined to object
Conscientiously

Letters came from "Nam"
As it was penned
One letter a week
And then
They stopped
Three years had come and gone
And those who went
Came home

I have no photos to depict
The blight of soldiers
Broken and spent
Back to America their lives to claim
But no parade gathered
To shout their names
No praise for years of shame
For a war long over before they came

There stood my Tom
In military poise
His soldier cap tucked under his arm
No wrinkle, no smudge
No sign of lint

But who is this stranger whose eyes
I met
The face it seems obscures my wit
The height I recall
The voice somewhat a bit too thick

His stride is broken to a limp
There are no teeth between his lips
Or laughter once so vividly

So who is he who thinks he knows
The ugly duckling he left back home
I reach for him
And he withdraws
Paralyzed to a pause
His actions eclipsed by memories
Frozen in time
He's back in Nam

Our past reduced to a stare
He's not there
So my sister
I console
For had she known
The epilogue
She wouldn't have stolen him at all

Now my boyfriend so full of charm
Was taken from her
By Vietnam

Whether fate or reciprocity
I do not know
I cannot decide
Whose heart was rent
Hers or mine
Only that life with all it holds
No portrait can capture
The scarring of soul

This is my ode
To the friend I lost
 to Vietnam

Breached

Usually
I come to you sealed
But not this time
The seal has been compromised
By the ravages of war
Moisture vulnerable to atmospheric pressures
Has all but destroyed my mission
Leaving my soul bare to public scrutiny
My heart exposed to the enemy
There is nothing sacred
In this place of death and toil
Not even the pages that reveal
 The fragile lives of those at war
Handle me with care
Caress me gingerly with your palms
Yearn for me in thought
I am the soul of the warrior in Vietnam

Last Letter from Vietnam

False light rises behind the sunset
The brook flows evenly with the rustic fields of
Morning quiet
Where Squadron 22 huddles in the trenches of war
Subtle movement saunters over the horizon of dawn
Pregnant with the promise of two nations
Both in anticipation of the other's demise

Gently I peel back the saliva sealed flap
That holds the hope of your survival
And how close you are to coming home
Lettered lines compose the chapters
Of a book written in the heat of battle
For once fresh joy wraps a rainbow
Around my thoughts

Then
Sudden dark clings fast to truculent skies
Grenades disrupt a thousand possibilities
Of a tomorrow at peace and

I can see the silhouette of a child
Amble listlessly across the path
Of camouflaged reality
Among whom your visage does not escape

My heart slows its pace
To honor your courage and patriotic strength

The pledge of a father
To return to his daughter unharmed
And husband love that holds secure
My waiting heart

 Now beating faster
To catch my racing fear
As the image draws near
I question the place of one so young
In the killing fields of adversarial fire
She can only be the age of our little Princess
Snoring peacefully
Next to her best friend doll
Ciana

I stride towards her
Hoping to rescue her
from an imminent nightmare

Which I pray is just a dream
Before she is trampled in a manic of gunfire
Or land mines booby trapped for enemies
Before her innocence lie naked upon the pages of history
Spattered with the blood of hatred

My eyes move frantically from word to word
Desperately searching her every move

If she dies
What would her trampling have served
Across the landscape of fallen dreams
And the Viet Cong fade into the gray
Of America history
There she is nearing you
My heart relaxes its rhythm of fear
For I am certain
She will be safe with you
That you will pull her out of the path of danger
And cover her as you would yours

But I am here
And she is there
And the blast is too loud
It blinds my searching for the child
Her limp body frail
With fluttering stands of curls

Now lying upon a heap of terrain
Camouflaged to hide grown men
Who watch for children
As they do enemies who transport death

Strapped around the loins of seedlings
They have born
Now sacrificed to war
And the duty of country

Soldier to soldier she cries
Then detonates
Before reaching your arms

I drop my head in anguish
Grief smitten anger
Then tears
Unrelenting

Mother tears
Wife tears
Sister and
Brother tears
The love of country tears
The hatred of war
Tears
As she folds into a mass
At the feet of a warrior
Fully geared to withstand attack
Pigtails twisted without resistance

Her smile unaffected by
Shrapnel unleashed by fury

Silence confirms her destiny
She's gone
With no balloons
Or confetti to announce her victory

She's gone
And no country will mourn
Not hers or mine
For you nor her

I cry
Blood tears
Between the lines of life and death
War
No peace
Sacrifice
No praise
I reach to comfort your distress
Your utter disillusionment with war

But I am here
And you are there
With her
Dead to history

Two soldiers linked to one epitaph
Whose names will ring no bell
None will toll the gate of hell
Nor petition heaven for your place

Sorrow bows to me
And I mount upon its wings

There is no comfort in knowing
Whether you died for your country or hers
Your love or mine
No one will ever know

For I am here
And you are there
With her
Breathless

Your last letter
 Creased between my sweaty palms
I tasted death for you and her
 Friend and foe
Your last words of ginger love
Will linger

I have just three more days
Before you are free to return

It doesn't much matter
How your story is told
Or if it ever is

If no one decorates your bravery
If no flag fly over your graves
However
If ever
Or perhaps never

You are
My hero
I shall remember that day
Two soldiers were slain
For the honor of country

I love you
I salute you
My soldier
My love

Words

Last night
I had the most poignant
Conversation to date
With Jennings
I clamped the right side
Of my brain
To silence analytical
Interference

As I mused through
The sound of his voice
Seeking integrity
Of character
Nobility of spirit
Agreement of soul

I heard him before
The familiarity
Of his contentment
The subtle touch of his manhood
Against my feminine wiles

He knew it
I knew it
Still, we continued
To navigate
The unchartered course
Unfolding before us

Believing perhaps
That something was happening
In that moment
Beyond our knowing
Or need to control

That's when I heard it
The rushing of wind words
From the core of my belly
I tried to push them back
But the flood
Would not recede

So I put my heart
On temporary pause
To listen with detached feelings
If that were possible

But, the symphony had already begun
The concert of three syllables
Eight letters
Three consonants
And three vowels
One noun
Holding it together
For two independent
Pronouns
Marching across
The bridge of tongue
Seeking voice
But finding none
I was not ready
It was not time
The spirit was willing
But I was not
So I whispered my prayer
Into the vacuum of thought
As the man read me like a card

I Long to Fall in Love with Love

I cannot fall in love
With skilled modulations
And metaphors
Before I can commit my heart
Lord, I must know

When I know
I shall love beyond
The haunting of the past
And hold some heart
In captive passion
And never leave him want again

Someday, somehow, someway
Someone
Will love me just as much
And then
Will hold my heart a mutual captive
And leave the past
It's own to fend
Until then
The road to there is hopeful

I dare not dim
Its guiding light
Someday, somehow
Someone and I
Will love the way
Our hearts desire

Exposed

Father
I can't hide
What you already know
The heart lie bare
You heard
You saw
The inner chambers
Of the woman exposed

Gingerly
He caressed me
Into a surrendered heap
A limp paper doll
Soul at peace

For a moment
In the arms
No time to think
No protest for honor
Or sanctified decree

Time passes quickly
A thousand memories flee
The widow twice abandoned
The lonely heart
Bereaved

One touch
One sudden
Tender stroke
Two intertwined in longing
No plan for saying no

Hold me
If but for a moment
In the passion of desire
For all the years of yearning
And love sacrificed
I offer no defense
Or recompense of silence
I was not seduced into submission
Or carnal compromise
Fully conscious of the moment
I consorted with my heart
So father forgive my indulgence
If that kiss was wrong

Love Unrequited is a Dream

May I record my thoughts
About love and lost?

I was to be with him
But could not
For in another life
I had taken what could never be
I crossed the line of principle
Wrought with fantasies
Borrowed from the other me
I partook in what was not
Those chained and bound
Pursued me as though free
And I cautioned my soul
Then paused
And resumed the folly of the chase

Then paused again
To listen to my heartbeat
Against my fleeing
I penned a letter
That never left my hand
No
I couldn't engage
The folly of soul

He was not mine
I was not his
For a time it went
As I had planned
But never a dream
Could I have dreamed
That desire not destroyed
Will rise again

So it was
The longing amid pain
That left my heart
Like driftwood
Floating upon waters
Without compass of soul
Except lost

There is none to blame
No finger to point
That does not return to me
I take full responsibility

It was I
Who at last
My own thoughts
I could not bear
The piteous footsteps
Upon my path

The reckless breathing of desire
The cause and effect
That renders the purest heart
Fallible

How and why
Does and can
The soul purge itself from sin?
Whether recorded here
Or concealed in thought
I cannot hide my heart
You are GOD

When Once I Loved

I've only loved twice in my life
Once
I am for sure
the other I just thought I loved
until I loved the one
I never dreamed to spend my years
to their blessed end
with but just one
whose love I frame
with mortal ink and pen
So tender
Gentle
was his touch
it still remains
unrivaled
And to his memory
I pledge this ode
though he
be not an idol
1996
Let history reverberate
I've only loved but one

let he who thought
himself so lucky
Guess who
He really was

Parker

You are the only one
Who I live to regret
Of not knowing how
To kiss your lips
How to hold your hand
in the desire of a soul
The only memory
That never grows old

The only one
Whose message to my heart
Leaves faded pages
Pressed together
By silent ink spots

Never to know
If we could have been
More than
Sixth grade friends

1-10-09

I was fifteen
The same night you proposed to me
Phillip gave me a ring
Parker wrote me a letter
And Charles Ray
Sent me a message by Ms Martha
My next door neighbor

I walked up Pender Street with Pap
Ten years my senior
Just to escape the tension to choose
Between men and boys
Playing gambling games
With my future

How could I know you were serious
Bracing yourself to be a man
Dashing
Self-confident
Assured

Hanging your high school pendant
Around my neck
And your senior ring upon my finger
For me pointed in no certain direction

But for you
Clearly declared your intentions

But I didn't see it

Did you ever forgive me
I knew nothing about life
Is it too late to say
I'm sorry

We met pulling beans
Or picking cotton
I don't remember
That's forty years lapse in memory

I couldn't do
What I didn't know
I couldn't give
What I didn't have

And I didn't have the nerves
To just say, No
I'm not the one
I can't go, or

So what if we're young
Let's go for it
So...
I did nothing

Just stood in silence
Wanting nothing more
Than to holler
Show me how
And I will go

I'm just a child

Barely in my teens

I can't see marriage

I can't breathe marriage

What do I know of love

What did you want from me

What did you want for me

I just didn't understand love
The way you seemed to know
Just what you wanted

Your mom and dad wanted the best for you
As did mine for me
So they came
To confirm your loyalty
To assure your uprightness
And husband worthiness

But I wasn't the one
I wasn't there
In that room

I was in a world far removed
Where a woman had stood
Eighteen years earlier
Pledging her love
On the side of the road
Saying
"I do...
"til death
To my dad

And the death
That had separated them
Was the death I feared

Infidelity
Breaching of the heart
Tossed and driven
To insanity

Was ours for real
Could love be ours
Forever and after
Vested in a hollow heart
Without surrender

Fearing
What I have reaped
Forty years wondering
Was he the one
Or just another
Toss of a coin
Or hopeful chancing
Perhaps

Maybe I would get lucky
And just like magic
We would waltz into a fantasy
But life was real
I just wasn't ready
To make that leap
From Oz
To reality

So I hid my heart
Behind living room curtains
And flirted
With those
I thought not as serious

I took Phillip's ring
Knowing all along
He was not a contender
So in a game of truth and dare

I chose the truth
I just wasn't ready
For a man like you

But every glance into the past
I often wished
I'd chosen dare

The Resolve

July 2010/ Composed a year later after you stopped speaking to me

Last night I saw you in a dream
Filled with anger
And accusing unable to shake the notion
That somehow I had betrayed you
Taken something from you
Refused to include you
Denied you your dream
Claimed what was yours
Except, it was mine
Your disheveled demeanor spoke volumes
What words could not say
Your image said it all
Your saddened presence
Covered the full spectrum of my dream
I approached but you were still cold
I hugged you with my eyes
And told you in truth unspoken
That I would not take anything from you
I'd already given you everything…

Then I awoke
To a new resolve
Leave me the hell alone
For I have no intentions
Of following you there

True Love Brings Tomorrow
The Manifesto of Ignorant Bliss

I love you very much today
But I'll wait to see what tomorrow brings
And yet I now in the strangest way
Tomorrow I'll love you more it seems
For behind each morn
Each noon and night
Through reveries dreams and endless sleep
I sense even then the flame glows bright
And the memories of the night to preserve and keep
I'll love you though love may cease to be
And when others doubt
I'll still believe
I love you very much today
And tomorrow true love won't fade away"

To whom did I speak
God or man
There were no suitors around the steps

At least not until
The following year
When all the tease and toss of words
Returned to require my love
As payment for attentiveness

Alonzo
Mintus
Phillip
And Fred
Rufus
Pap
Charles
And Ed

Seeking the fantasies of a pseudonym
Sprawled across the hearts of men
As "The Spoiler"
Writing my way into the world
Where I was permitted to dream
About what was not

Until at last and then I fought
To lock away the thirst
That words had so fully quenched
Among the draught of dark
And desolate dismay

Where I gave birth
To the glorious cadence
And sway of bibliography
That refused to wane

Through parable
And paradox
Myth and
Metaphor
Iambic and
Pentameter
Mystery
And lore

Amid fantasy and farce
In the shadows of the forgotten
I was born again
From the belly of a narrative
With rhyme
And rhythm
Free verse
And form

I picked up pencil
And pen
And rewrote my story
Until the wells of vastness
Unformed
Busted forth
To unleash the me
God Born

No longer hidden
behind enigmatic metaphors

I Write Poems

Now
I write poems
but only to those I feel strongly about
Those whose lives
unmistakably
touched mine
and mine theirs

I write poems
But not just to anyone
I write to that special someone
who makes me laugh
when my heart is aching
and I need to cry

Someone who knows
the value of a friend
the joy of a smile
the comfort of a cry

To him I write
not because I am a great poet
but because he is a poem
being created
line by line
for what he has become in my heart

Unchained

2/14/2012

An invitation
To a Buck's game
A text of a single
Red rose
Two brief conversations
To say "thank-you"
I love you
Withheld
Hovering
Apprehensively
In the atmosphere
Clinging to the fear
Of rejection
And deformed manhood
Hurt
Wounds still opened
Scar tissue
Exposed to scrutiny

Love just a fable
For fools
A chance encounter
Between strangers
Or past hearts
Now estranged

Separated by offenses
Not easily forgotten
Valentines
Turned vexation
Love abandoned
Without possibility
Of renewal
No second chances
No rewrites
Love turned
Hate
Excuses abused
Time out used
Apologies
Mistaken for stupidity
Silence
But not serenity
Surrender
But not victory

Compromise
But not cowardice
Lonely
But not alone
Heart aching
But not broken
Disappointed
But not devastated
Shaken
But not shattered

Life force
Threatened
But still intact
Confidence tested
But not eroded
Hope still clings to faith
Faith still
Working by love
Love remains
The greatest of all
Human
And
Divine encounters

It has taken some learning
Some purging
Of fallacies
Intense difficulties
And extraordinary
Challenges
To birth this certainty

I have but one
True valentine
One eternal flame
That will never
Be extinguished
By pain
Or comfort

Happiness
Or sorrow
Failure
Or success
Weariness
Of spirit
Rest
Or toil
Triumph
Or tragedy
Fame
Or infamy
Wealth
Or poverty

His love is
Unconditional
His character
Unimpeachable
His promise
Inviolable
His phone
Never busy
He's always reachable
So as long as
I do not break
The communion
His grace abounds
His loyalty
Unquestionable

His word is a tower
His tongue
Speaks his justice

Committed to truth
He cannot lie
When he says
"I love you"
It's infallible
Immutable
An indisputable truth

No hidden agenda
Or ulterior motives
He's not being deceitful
Or trying to control me
It's real
Take it to the bank
No greater love
Than his
To speak of
Gentle
Kind
Alms giving
Compassionate
Leading
Constructive counsel
Abounding
In wisdom

Anchored
In forgiveness
Constant
in mercy
Driven by purpose
Not swayed by conventions
Undeterred by trouble
Loving
Loyal
Community builder
His arm not short
His ears not heavy
Protector of children
Honoring women
Hated for his perfection
Scorned for his courage
In him I ascend
To the greatness
I was born for
Beyond mediocre
To my highest potential
Free to live
My purest convictions

Doris Wellington

Former American University student and North Carolina native; Doris Wellington, is an ordained minister, spiritual life strategist, public speaker, dream analyst, and visionary writer.

Doris Wellington has effectively interwoven and branded a wide range of products, services and innovative ideas that bridge the power and potential of spirit, soul and body. "Without this triumphant interaction, we would never understand nor could we ever apply the full range of our God-given abilities." Recognizing that the grace of our gifts comes from God, **Doris Wellington** delivers life changing spiritual, motivational, and educational conferences, media, theatre, and visionary business concepts and creative ideas.

She has authored, twenty epic stage plays, including the celebrated allegorical production, I Waltzed with God the Morning of
Genesis: A Mosaic for Peace,, Dead Woman Dancing on Her Grave, and God, I'm Here and I'm Colored: the National Debate on Race and Equality. She is the author of the thirteen-book poetic epistolary, Romancing God: The Divine Love Affair; as well as The Divine Notebook: Letters and The Poverty Manifesto.

Additionally, she has authored four novels, and one memoir, The River God Runs through Her. She coauthored, Stokestown: Dreaming behind Closed Doors., 2015. She has recorded and studied more than 20 000 prophetic dreams, visions and supernatural visitations. She founded and wrote the curriculum for **The Prophetic Path Dream Summit**, which teaches the prophetically inclined how to tap into the hidden power of dreams.

Dwelling Places Worldwide
Home of Books and Letters
By Doris Wellington

Amazon.com

I Waltzed with God the Morning of Genesis
Romancing God: the Divine Love Affair, Volumes 1-8
Romancing God: Memoirs of a Worshipper, Volumes 1-8
Stokestown: Dreaming behind Closed Doors
The River God Runs through Her: Praise for an unlikely Champion
Pastoral Letters: the Essential Collection
Studies in Prayer, Volumes 1-8
Tell Me Your Truth, I'll Sell You My Lie: behind the Veil of Santa Claus
The Night before Christ in the Battle for Christmas
Behind Enemy Lines: Strategist Weapons of Spiritual Warfare Sleep Dream
Sleep, Dream, Become: Understanding the World You Dream
God, I'm Here and I'm Colored: the National Debate on Race & Equality
Feat Songs of Protest and National Pride

Coming Soon!!!

Chronicles of a Woman: An Epic Celebration of Woman in Full
Titles in Series Include the following

First, I am Woman: the Purpose, Power and Praise of Womanhood
Woman of God become Thyself
Dead Woman Dancing on Her Grave: Unstoppable
The Dear John Reader: Rituals of Disclosure in Love
and Emotional Emancipation
Rhapsody for September: Love Letters

Woman in a Jar: Narratives of an Imperfect Sanity
The Hurt Café: How to Have a Breakdown without Going Crazy
The Hurt Café, Volume 2:
Narratives of Abuse and the Abdication of Shame
The Hurt Café, Volume 3: Healing for Wounded Warriors
The autobiography of Poverty: My Life in Poem

First Lady, Last Victim
The Gift of Flesh
Stokestown: Dreaming behind Closed Doors
The River God Runs through Her: Praise for an unlikely Champion
One Summer in London: Songs and Sonnets for Levi
If Coffee Could Talk, It Would Hold a Press Conference
Woman: Inequities & Ambiguities: Selected Writings
Seven Letters to Seven Fellows: In Praise of a Good Man

Dwelling Places

WORLDWIDE

A Publisher of Books & Letters